Dream Big Henry!

by Barbara Bradley

Illustrated by Jean Barlow

WARREN PUBLISHING, INC.

The Brain Recovery Project

Published by Warren Publishing, Inc.
Charlotte, NC
www.warrenpublishing.net

ISBN: 978-0-9908136-5-1
Library of Congress Control Number: 2014956247

For Billy, Nathan, my buddy, Katie, my little bug
...and Henry, of course.

Acknowledgements

At the age of two, my daughter Katie began having seizures. After her rare diagnosis, we began an unexpected journey that eventually lead to two brain surgeries. A procedure called a hemispherectomy is a drastic option but it became Katie's only option. We are grateful for the surgery, but new challenges arise after the incision heals, and the doctors don't send you home with an instruction manual. For Katie and others like her, knowledge is power. That knowledge comes from research...and more research.

A portion of the proceeds of this book will go to a foundation started by Brad and Monika Jones, fellow parents of a child like my Katie. Their dedication to helping their son Henry and the rest of us battling this lifelong fight to recovery for our children is unmatched. **The Brain Recovery Project** is paving the way for our children's future by funding groundbreaking research to help write that "instruction manual" on how to rehabilitate children like Katie and Henry so they both can Dream Big!

One week ago, a summer breeze carried Henry and his whole family to a fence post that overlooked Grassy Meadow. Now, it was his new home.

And today was his first day to start second grade at Grassy Meadows Elementary School.

"Are you ready?" asked his mother, anxiously. She moved quickly, packing his lunch box and checking his book bag.

"You're making me nervous, Mom," said Henry, pushing his eyeglasses up to the bridge of his nose as he and his mother peered out the window. They were waiting for the bus to take him to school.

Just then, a huge dragonfly flapped her wings outside the window. "Grassy Meadows! Next stop!"

Henry's mother helped him strap his wheelchair onto the dragonfly's back.

"I'm Henry," he introduced himself.

"You can call me Doris," said the dragonfly. "Hold on tight!"

Henry held on as Doris zoomed straight down in a dizzying blur right onto the front steps of Grassy Meadows Elementary. Ready or not, his first day at his new school had begun.

The name above the door announced: "Ms. Flutter's: Second Grade Classroom". Inside the door were all types of bugs: ladybugs, grasshoppers, caterpillars, grubs, beetles...

Henry carefully wheeled inside the room. He looked down and slowed his wheelchair to a stop at Ms. Flutter's desk.

She smiled and said gently, "Welcome to our classroom, Henry. Class, say hello to Henry. He is new to Grassy Meadows." She lifted her beautiful, blue wings and they fluttered in the breeze.

Henry thought he heard whispers as he passed the other students sitting at their desks. *"What's wrong with him? Why is he in a chair? He looks different."* He kept on rolling. He was embarrassed. A brown moth and a fuzzy caterpillar giggled as he rolled past. Bryn the stinkbug and Mel the dung beetle pinched their noses.

Henry kept rolling to the only empty desk, next to a bright green grasshopper.

He smiled at Henry and said, "Hi! My name is Nathan."

Ms. Flutter handed out lots of classwork and Henry was so busy, he missed the lunch bell warning to finish up. He was slower than the others. When he finally made his way to the lunchroom, the other students were already out of the line and saving seats for their friends. Nathan motioned for Henry to join him.

"Hey, Henry, over here. Sit with me!" the grasshopper called.

He had made a friend. It was a good day!

The rest of the week went by quickly. Henry grew accustomed to his new classroom and even made a few more friends.

By the second week, Henry couldn't even remember what it had been like at his old school. He knew where to find all the handout materials, the books and the markers, the lunchroom, and even the auditorium.

One day, during recess, Ms. Flutter made an announcement.

"We are having our first ever Grassy Meadows Elementary School musical. I expect everyone to participate. We will need dancers, singers, and musicians."

The class was abuzz.

"I'll sing," cried Mel, the dung beetle.

"I'm going to dance," said Katie, the ladybug, as she jumped around, spinning and twirling.

"I can play the flute," chimed in Ollie, the roly poly.

Everyone was so happy. They were shouting and laughing.

"Quiet down," cautioned Ms. Flutter.

But Henry wasn't happy. He couldn't sing and he certainly couldn't dance.

Nathan could tell Henry was upset.

"Don't worry, Henry. We will find a part for you. Everybody is good at something," his friend said. "Maybe you can play an instrument."

The next day Nathan and Henry visited the music teacher, Mr. Harp.

"Give these a try Henry. You can even borrow one to take home and practice if you would like." said Mr. Harp.

Henry tried the guitar, the drums, the trumpet, and a saxophone but nothing seemed to work for him.

Back in class, Henry doodled a beautiful drawing on his math paper and Ms. Flutter saw it while she was collecting their work.

"Henry, may I speak with you after class?" she asked.

Before heading home, Ms. Flutter shared her idea with Henry about how he could help out with the musical. Henry was so excited.

After school, Henry rushed home to his mom. "Mom! Guess what, guess what, guess what!"

"Slow down, son. What is it?" his mother asked. It had been a tough month, so she was pleased to see Henry in a good mood for a change.

In a burst of excitement, Henry shared the events of the day and his part in the school musical. He asked if he could eat his dinner early so he could get to work. After all, Henry had a lot to accomplish between now and opening night.

The night of the musical Henry sat nervously between his mom and dad. Even though his part was done, he couldn't seem to relax. The room went quiet when the lights were dimmed and the curtains were drawn. The stage glowed with the silhouette of skyscrapers.

While his classmates rehearsed singing and dancing, Henry had been busy drawing and painting the set. From the street signs and taxis to the busy storefronts and cafes, he had designed every detail of the background for the performers to tell the story.

As the musical came to a close, Ms. Flutter entered the stage again and thanked the performers and crew. Then, she thanked Henry.

"Let's give our stagehand, Henry, a special round of applause for designing our set. There are no small parts. Everyone here did their part to make this first musical a success!"

From the stage, under the bright spotlights, Henry could see everyone in the audience standing and cheering their thanks, gratitude, and well-wishes. And there, in the front row, Henry could see and hear his mom and dad most of all. His dad winked and gave him a thumbs-up while his mom clapped loudly, a big smile on her face. Henry knew just what she was thinking; *"Henry, you are my very special spider."*

It was a night Henry would remember always.

The End

About the Author

Photo by Abbey Ritter

Barbara Bradley is a Texas native living in North Carolina with her husband Billy and their two children, Nathan and Katie. She majored in journalism but worked in the corporate setting after graduation and remained until having her second child. Life took a different path after her daughter was diagnosed with a rare brain malformation called hemimegalencephaly. When Katie began suffering from seizures and her condition worsened, Barbara began journaling to keep family and friends updated. The journaling rekindled her love for writing. This is her first book.

About the Illustrator

Jean Barlow, illustrator of *Dream Big Henry!* holds an Associate Degree in Art from the Art Institute of Pittsburgh. She retired as a reading tutor in 2011. She now illustrates and does decorative painting. Jean is married to Ron Barlow, and they have one son, Eric.

CPSIA information can be obtained at www.ICGtesting.com
Printed in the USA
BVOW11*1718220115

384258BV00007B/3/P